Authority

Deal with it before it deals with you

Anne Marie Aikins • Illustrated by Steven Murray

James Lorimer & Company Ltd., Publishers
Toronto

If you could be your own boss,

life would be great, wouldn't it?

You could do whatever you wanted and wouldn't have to listen to anyone. No bedtime or curfew, no rules to follow, no lectures from adults who don't listen. And you would never get in trouble for talking back!

You already know that life is never going to be like that. There will always be people making choices for you. When you're a kid, it seems like everyone is older and has more say than you about how to live your life. But guess what? It doesn't change much as you get older. No matter who you are, you can't avoid dealing with people in authority.

People in authority have the right to make decisions about your life and behaviour.

So what gives someone the right to tell you what you can or cannot do? Imagine a classroom with no teacher, or a home without parents or guardians. Think about how unsafe the streets would be without police controlling traffic and enforcing laws. It might seem like it would be fun to do whatever you feel like, but people in authority help make your community, home, or classroom safe and fair.

Does that mean you're locked into always doing whatever other people tell you?

It's a sign of growing up to be rebellious and want to challenge your parents or teachers. And sometimes people in authority make mistakes. Authority is based on respect — not fear — and respect is a two-way street. So learning how to challenge authority respectfully is as important as respecting someone you may have authority over.

If you have trouble dealing with authority, reading this book will be the first step towards changing that.

Contents

Who's the Boss?

Okay, so you know who's in charge, right?

It's your mom and dad, or a teacher or police officer. Yup, everyone knows you have to listen to those people. There are many adults who may have some authority over you, like

the bus driver

your doctor

your grandparents

your friends' parents

a guidance counsellor

a security officer

a religious or community leader

Often, when there is a disagreement between an adult and a kid, what the adult says goes. But how about people closer to your own age? What about:

your older brother or sister?

your tennis instructor?

your scout leader?

the captain of your soccer team?

a crossing guard?

a babysitter?

Are these people in authority? They are when they have the power to make choices and decisions for you.

People are *given* authority

because they are...

QUIZ

Having trouble figuring out whether someone is exercising their authority or just using power to get their way? Keep this in mind: authority means (1) a person is responsible for you, and (2) that the person is guiding, teaching, protecting, or placing fair limits on you. Decide whether each of the following situations is an example of a person using authority or power. Check your answers on the following page.

1 Sassy Sister

Sheila's older sister hates the way Sheila dresses, and yells at her to stop dressing like a boy.

2 Unfair Ref

Jerry thinks the referee in his soccer game is being unfair, so he doesn't think he should have to listen to him.

3 Friendly Advice

Matthew and Pete are best friends. Matthew thinks that Pete's mother doesn't treat Pete fairly. She's always yelling and complaining, and Matthew thinks Pete should tell her off.

4 Dance Distress

The dance monitor keeps yelling at Patti to clean up the mess in the bathroom, even though Patti is not on the clean-up committee.

5 Rude Encounter

Freddie thinks the man behind the counter at the burger shop has shortchanged him. He starts shouting and calling the man names.

6 Ignorant Adolescent

When Ann's mom tells her to do her homework, Ann just ignores her.

9 Rough Rider

The crossing guard tells Kareem to walk his bike across the street. Since she's younger than he is, Kareem just tells her to shut up and rides across the street.

7 Bossy Best Bud

Jabari is small for his age and his friend Terrance is older and much bigger. Terrance likes to order Jabari around.

10 Anger Issues

Beth catches her friend Aisha kissing her ex-boyfriend Sam. Beth insists that Aisha has to apologize to her, and she demands that Sam never go near Aisha again.

8 Back Talker

Jose is rude and mouthy to his scout leader. The guy isn't much older than Jose, and never says anything when he's a smart mouth.

Answers

1. Power. Sheila's sister doesn't have authority over Sheila's clothing choices. It looks like she's trying to force her style on Sheila just to prove that she can.
2. Authority. Jerry may disagree, but ultimately the referee must be allowed to control the game.
3. Authority. It's hard for Matthew to put his feelings aside, but it's important for him to respect Pete's mother's authority. As a friend, what he should do is be available and supportive of Pete if he needs someone to talk to.
4. Power. Patti should tell the dance monitor that it is her not her responsibility to clean up the mess, and find a teacher if she continues to bully her.
5. Authority. Freddie shouldn't talk back to the man, even if he thinks he was ripped off. If there is a dispute over change, he should try to work it out in a respectful way.
6. Authority. Ann's mother is trying to help her learn. Ann's behaviour is very rude and disrespectful of her mother's authority.
7. Power. Terrance is attempting to use fear and intimidation to get Jabari to do what he wants, whether or not it is in Jabari's best interests.
8. Authority. The other kid has been given the responsibility of leading the scout team, so Jose should respect his authority.
9. Authority. The crossing guard has been given the authority to make sure people crossing the street are safe. For his own safety, Kareem should respect her authority.
10. Power. It is an upsetting situation for Beth, but she doesn't have authority over Aisha or Sam.

Dear Authority Counsellor

Q: I get that my parents are responsible for me at home and my teacher is in charge at school. And the police are the boss of everybody, I guess. But there are all these other people who are older, or who just always tell me what to do. Why does everyone have power over me?

— Powerless

A: Sometimes it can be frustrating to deal with all the people in authority. But it's not about power. People in authority are there to help guide and teach you. If you're not sure that someone wants the best for you, you are responding out of fear instead of respect. Remember there are lots of areas in your life where you can make decisions and choices. Try to look at each person in authority as an individual. If your feelings continue, talk to your parents or a guidance counsellor.

Q: Sometimes my teachers treat me really unfairly. I don't think I should be forced to listen to them if they are wrong. Shouldn't I speak up when they are being unfair?

— Fighting for Fairness

A: It's great that you want to protect your rights. Challenging authority when it is wrong takes a lot of guts. But you have to choose the right time and place to speak up — and do so with respect and without anger. Backtalk never works. Sometimes it's helpful to get support from others when challenging people in authority. Ask a trusted adult to help you develop a strategy.

Q: There aren't a whole lot of rules at our house. My parents are easygoing and encourage us to speak our minds. It works well for us, but now I don't really know how to handle authority. Can't I get through life just doing what I decide is best for me?

— Free to be Me

A: It sounds like you are a very independent person and that's great! But you may not be able to see all the ways your parents have influenced your life. Everyone, even adults, must answer to someone else — bosses, the police, their elders, and other more experienced people. Look carefully at the direction your life has taken and how it was guided by your family. Maybe you're more comfortable with authority than you think!

Q: My parents are very strict and I wouldn't dare talk back to them. I'd get in a lot of trouble for speaking my mind. How can I get my parents to back off a little?

— Good Kid

A: Sometimes parents think their children need to be strictly controlled, and they use punishments to discourage bad behaviour. Prove to them that you are trustworthy and responsible — show them that you respect their authority. Talk to your parents about negotiating the rewards and punishments in your family.

Q: I signed up for the dance committee and somehow got chosen as the chairperson. But I'm really not sure what that means. Why does someone have to be in charge?

— Squeamish

A: Committees are formed to get a job done, and the chairperson is appointed to ensure that happens. For example, one of your tasks might be booking committee meetings. It's much easier to do this when one person is keeping track of everyone else's schedule. But being chairperson doesn't mean you should intimidate people or boss them around. Use your responsibilities wisely and your committee should be able to put on a great dance! You'll earn a lot of respect, too.

Myths

Talking tough makes people in authority back down.

Some people in authority back down to smart-mouths, but most of the time talking back just creates problems.

Someday I won't have to answer to anyone in authority.

Even adults have people who make decisions for them, and problems when they rebel against authority.

People in authority have all the power.

Authority is about respect and power is based on fear. You have a choice in how to respond to people who try to influence your life or behaviour.

Did You Know?

- People obey authority out of respect, while they obey power out of fear.

Talking back to a stranger doesn't hurt anyone.

Disrespecting any person in authority, even a stranger, can get you a reputation as a troublemaker.

Fighting people in authority will ensure no one takes advantage of you.

Unlike bullies, most people in authority are looking out for your interests. Rebelling just for rebellion's sake is no way to protect your rights.

Rebellion is a sign of a strong character.

It's never that simple. For example, mouthing off is a sign of disrespect and blinds people to your good qualities.

- Negotiating with authority figures is a skill that must be learned over time.
- People who have had bad experiences with authority may see rebellious behaviour as a means of gaining control.

Nobody is the boss of you!

You're the player who yells at the coach when she tries to tell you what to do. Or the one who tunes out when your dad tries to teach you something. Or maybe you make fun of the sales clerks at the mall when they try to keep you from making a mess of their store.

And what's wrong with being a rebel, anyway? Some of the coolest people in history are the ones who refused to obey the people in charge.

You're right: just because some people challenge authority, it doesn't mean they're bad. But problems with authority could get out of control when your rebellion puts the safety and rights of others at risk.

Think about it: why do you always push back? There could be a number of reasons:

- You have had a bad experience with a person in authority.
- You haven't had much experience with limits or guidance.
- You've experienced someone misusing power.
- Your family is really strict.
- You're looking for attention.
- You're upset or concerned about something.
- You distrust people, especially adults.
- You've gotten away with being a smart-mouth.
- You are following the example of someone else.
- You've just gotten into the habit of talking back.

Whatever the reason, it's never too late to change. You can learn to respond in another way — a way that doesn't cause you grief.

do's and don'ts

✓ Do remember that most people in authority are trying to help you.

✓ Do realize that you don't have to be perfect. Everyone makes mistakes.

✓ Do speak to your parents or another trustworthy adult.

✓ Do think before you speak. Take a few minutes to calm down. Breathe.

✓ Do believe it's never too late to change.

✓ Do try to adjust your attitude about authority. Think about the reasons you automatically rebel.

✓ Do practise self-control. You have the power.

✓ Do ask for help.

✓ Do look for good role models.

✓ Do use your courage to change.

✓ Do find friends who respect authority.

✗ Don't let backtalk become a habit.

✗ Don't hate the world and yourself.

✗ Don't try to solve the problem all by yourself. Get help.

✗ Don't give up on all authority figures just because you have trouble with one.

✗ Don't let your anger make others stop taking you seriously.

QUIZ

Rebel with or without a cause?

Are you standing up for your rights or only looking out for yourself? When does defying authority become dangerous rebellion? Take this quiz and see what you can find out. Of the following statements, how many are true, how many false?

1. I have been called a smart-mouth.
2. When I don't want to do something, I shout at people.
3. I hate people telling me what to do.
4. I like feeling a bit out of control.
5. I get into trouble at school for not listening.
6. Lots of people don't deserve respect.
7. Nobody should have the right to boss another person around.
8. I'm good at giving attitude.
9. I get into trouble at home a lot.

I get into a lot of arguments. **10**

I know what's best for me better than anyone else does. **11**

All my heroes are "bad guys." **12**

I like getting a reaction from people. **13**

I feel better after taking my anger out on others. **14**

I want people to think I'm tough. **15**

I try to get out of class whenever I can. **16**

I don't like responsibility. **17**

I'm bad at following through on promises. **18**

I have trouble trusting people. **19**

People don't understand me. **20**

I don't understand why I have to respect people just because I'm told to. **21**

Did you score a lot of trues? Maybe it's time to start thinking about trusting and respecting people, and to talk to someone about why you always have to fight against authority.

There are some basic things you can do

to chill out and be reasonable when it comes to authority.

Explore Your Feelings

Ask yourself why are you so uncomfortable with authority. Does it make you feel angry or powerless when someone tells you what to do? There are always reasons behind our actions, and there are usually payoffs or consequences. What are yours?

Be honest with yourself

Who do you give lip to most often? Do you lash out when you are angry or frustrated about something? Or do you rebel to get attention? It's really difficult to change yourself if you haven't figured out the patterns in the way you act.

Examine the consequences

How much trouble have you gotten into for not co-operating with people in authority? Has it made your life simpler? Has it even gotten the result you were looking for? It might be helpful for you to discuss this with a trusted adult, like a guidance counsellor.

Use your voice wisely

Being outspoken isn't a bad thing — it means you are willing to take risks. That's good, except when it gets you into trouble. Find ways to show you're unique and to take risks that don't depend on defying people in authority. Learn to compromise.

DID YOU KNOW?

- Studies have found that teens appreciate limits to help them make wise choices.
- Taking risks and challenging authority is part of growing up.

When Power is Involved

People in authority have a responsibility to make the right decisions for other people. But sometimes people in authority misuse their positions. For example, when an adult tries to get a child involved with sex, it's sexual abuse — and it's wrong. Some people use negative behaviours like discrimination, physical abuse, or bullying to get someone to do what they want. This is really about power, not authority.

If you have ever experienced something like this, it's important for you to remember:

- It's not your fault.
- You didn't deserve it.
- You are not alone.
- You must tell someone, even if it happened a long time ago.

Think before you act
Speak up about the things that are bothering you and learn the skill of negotiating. When angry, take a deep breath and give yourself a few minutes to cool down.

Every person in authority — even police officers, teachers, and parents — might at times use their power in ways that only benefit themselves. When people misuse positions of authority, it's okay to challenge them. Use your instincts and listen to your gut when deciding if the person is trying to take advantage of you. Stand up for yourself, even if you find it hard to do.

Here are some suggestions:

- Stay calm, cool, and collected.
- Get help. Speak to someone you trust.
- Think about your safety first. Do whatever it takes to keep safe.
- Go along with the person's orders if absolutely necessary in order to stay safe, but get out of the situation and get help as fast as you can. Confronting someone isn't always the safest way to handle every situation. It may be better to let someone speak for you.
- Explore all your options. Make an informed choice.
- If you do speak up, use a clear, loud voice. Tell the power-tripper to stop or you will tell someone.
- Don't remain silent. If you have been abused, talk to a counsellor or someone else who can help. No one deserves to be hurt like that, and it's important that you speak up.
- Call the police.
- Explore the complaints process at school.
- If you're not sure what to do, speak with a counsellor.

- Mouthing off in the classroom makes learning difficult because it distracts everyone.
- Respect for parents is highly valued in every culture.
- 80% of child abuse is committed by a person in authority.

Hey, you're just a kid.

There must be a good reason why so many people can tell you what to do. Everyone needs guidance, right? And the best way to stay out of trouble is to do exactly what you're told. Sure, you're easily intimidated and sometimes get taken advantage of or pushed around. So what? Besides, someday you'll be the one who everyone obeys. There's nothing wrong with always co-operating with the people in charge.

Or is there?

DEAR DR. SHRINK-WRAPPED . . .

Q: My best friend's father is always rude to me when I come around. He often says nasty things about my family. I don't want to be disrespectful because I know it will just make things worse. But saying nothing makes me burn inside. How should I handle it when a person in authority acts unfairly?

— Burning for Fairness

A: It sounds to Dr. Shrink-Wrapped like you are trying hard to respect authority. Good for you. But you also expect to be treated fairly and with respect, which is good, too. When you feel authority is being misused, try these approaches:

- Continue being well-behaved and respectful.
- Spend some time getting to know your friend's father.
- Help him get to know and to trust you.
- Politely ask your friend's father if you have done something to offend him.
- Get some advice about the situation from people you trust.
- Walk away when faced with rudeness or disrespect.
- Practise being assertive in front of the mirror.
- When challenging a person in authority, it helps to have support by your side.
- If nothing works, try avoiding your friend's father as much as possible while remaining supportive of your friend.
- Remember, you can't change anyone except yourself.

Q: Ever since my teacher made me class monitor my friends accuse me of bossing everyone around. I don't want to lose my friends, but I don't want to give up my job, either. How do I handle being in charge?

— First-timer

A: Dr. Shrink-Wrapped thinks you are up to the challenge of taking on a position of authority in your class. Try the following strategy:

- Ask you teacher to outline your duties and responsibilities as class monitor.
- Make sure both you and the rest of your class understand why it's necessary to have a class monitor.
- Try to be fair and consistent — don't make exceptions for your friends.
- Use your authority without being bossy, abusive, or rude.
- When your classmates accuse you of being bossy, try not to be defensive. Listen carefully to what they are saying and consider whether they may be right or whether they are simply trying to get out of trouble.
- Share the duties — ask your teacher to set a time limit so the role can be shared by other classmates.

The **Co-operator**

QUIZ

There are basically three ways you can choose to handle authority. You can always go along with it, no matter what (Pushover). You can speak your mind if the person in charge is being unreasonable or unfair (Future Leader). Or you can take the side of whoever has authority, and try to get some of that power for yourself (Tyrant-in-Training). Take this quiz and then check on the opposite page to see how you respond to authority.

1 Sound Argument

You're having a great time at home with your friends listening to music and laughing. The neighbours in the next apartment start banging on the walls, complaining about the noise. Do you: a) Turn off the music? b) Go to the neighbours and tell them you will turn the music down, but you would like to continue listening? c) Start yelling at your friends and kick them out?

2 POPULAR PREZ

The president of the student council, a really popular kid, bullies and bosses Jamal around every time they meet up in the hallway. Does Jamal: a) Put up with it? Someday, he'll be in a position to tell others what to do. b) Hide out in the washroom whenever he sees the bully coming toward him? c) Ask the bully why he's giving him such a hard time, and speak with a teacher or the principal?

3 WORKING THE NUMBERS

You need some extra help with math, so your teacher assigns you a tutor. Half the time the tutor never shows up, and he asks you to keep quiet about it. Do you: a) Tell the guy that you really need the help, and that if he can't make it you'll ask your teacher for another tutor? b) Just forget about it? c) Lie to your teacher and say that the tutor is doing a great job?

4 SCREAMING SISTER

You're babysitting your little sister. Your parents said she had to go right to bed, but she wants you to take her out, and throws a temper tantrum. Do you: a) Give in and take your sister out to make her stop screaming? b) Tell her that you are in charge and lock her in her room? c) Tell her that your parents expect you both to be good, and offer to read her an extra bedtime story?

5 Bowling for Attitude

The man who runs the bowling alley keeps giving you attitude because your friend Nathalie once mouthed off to him. Do you: a) Stop going to the bowling alley? b) Tell him politely that you haven't given him a reason to treat you this way? c) Make a big deal of yelling at Nathalie for ruining it for everyone?

6 GARBAGE IN, GARBAGE OUT

The superintendent of your apartment building asks you to help put the garbage pails out to the road. Do you: a) Tell him you'd be glad to help if you're around? b) Change your schedule so you can include it in your chores? c) Bully your little brother into doing it?

7 SOCCER CHALLENGE

Your soccer coach pushes your team really hard, and you find his passion for the sport intimidating. Do you: a) Put down your teammates for not playing well enough? b) Try to relax and appreciate the effort your coach is making to build a great team? c) Change to a different team?

8 CURFEW FEUD

Your dad has set a strict early curfew for you, and you often miss out on all the fun with your friends. Do you: a) Go home when you are supposed to? b) Tell your friends that their parents obviously don't care about them, and that they should head home at the same time you do? c) Speak to your dad and try to negotiate a fairer curfew?

Answers

1.	a) Pushover b) Future Leader c) Tyrant-in-Training	5.	a) Pushover b) Future Leader c) Tyrant-in-Training	9.	a) Pushover b) Future Leader c) Tyrant-in-Training
2.	a) Tyrant-in-Training b) Pushover c) Future Leader	6.	a) Future Leader b) Pushover c) Tyrant-in-Training	10.	a) Tyrant-in-Training b) Future Leader c) Pushover
3.	a) Future Leader b) Pushover c) Tyrant-in-Training	7.	a) Tyrant-in-Training b) Future Leader c) Pushover		
4.	a) Pushover b) Tyrant-in-Training c) Future Leader	8.	a) Pushover b) Tyrant-in-Training c) Future Leader		

9 Teacher Tantrum

Your teacher is a screamer. He yells every command and seems angry all the time. You're new to this country, and this kind of behaviour makes you very uncomfortable. Do you: a) Try not to make him angry? b) Deal with it by speaking with the guidance counsellor? c) Yell back, as this must be the way things are done here?

10 Bus Business

You get on the bus with a group of friends, and you're the first in line. The bus driver questions your student pass, taking a long time scrutinizing it and you. Do you: a) Check your friends' passes and tell him which ones have expired? b) Ask him politely if there is a problem with your pass? c) Just wait, but curse him in your head?

The **Co-operator**

How to
a Better

The best way to be a better co-operator is to accept authority when it makes things better for everyone, and to question it when it seems to be denying someone their rights or safety. Being a better co-operator will make you a better friend, team member, and leader. There are many things you can do to increase the amount of respect you show and receive:

Examine how you feel about people in authority. Do they intimidate you? Do you envy them? Would you like to be in charge so you could intimidate others? What are you afraid will happen if you say what's on your mind?

Build up your self-esteem. Look for ways to feel good about yourself. The more confident you are, the less likely it is that you will be a pushover, reducing your need to feel in control of other people.

Be a good leader. Just as people in authority who act unfairly might not deserve your respect, you can't impose what you want on other people just because you have followed the rules.

Did You Know?

- Parents have a legal duty to give their children the "necessities of life" until the age of 16.

Be Co-operator

Learn from authority figures. What do you think are the qualities that make a good leader? Consider who your role models are and why. What mistakes have you observed people in authority making that you can learn from?

do's and don'ts

- ✓ Do use your voice. Speak up.
- ✓ Do think about your feelings, especially your fears — real and imagined.
- ✓ Do look for ways to challenge unfair people.
- ✓ Do get to know yourself and what you want in life.
- ✓ Do use your determination.
- ✓ Do work on feeling comfortable with expressing yourself.
- ✓ Do relax and stop putting so much pressure on yourself.
- ✓ Do consider others if you find yourself in a position of authority.

- ✗ Don't worry so much.
- ✗ Don't be judgmental.
- ✗ Don't be afraid of authority.
- ✗ Don't panic if you make a mistake.
- ✗ Don't give up trying to make improvements.
- ✗ Don't blindly obey people in authority if you feel they are wrong.
- ✗ Don't expect others to obey you just because you think you're the boss.

- "Necessities of life" for children include clothing, shelter, medical care, and education.
- Anyone who suspects a child is being neglected or abused is required by law to report it.

Have you ever been around when a friend confronted someone in authority?

What about when power was misused? Did you speak up? Did you make it clear that you didn't think it was cool? Did you do anything at all? Well, why not?

You do have a choice!

do's and don'ts

✓ Do educate yourself about authority. Learn to be comfortable with speaking up.

✓ Do learn about choices. Be decisive.

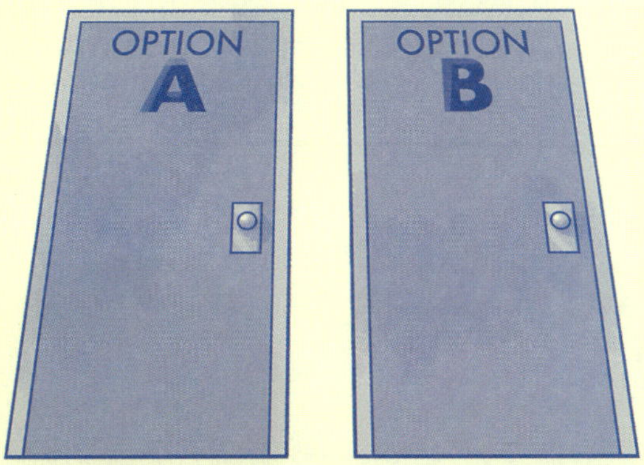

✓ Do use your voice. Get involved and be supportive.

✓ Do talk to a trustworthy adult.

✓ Do get help — a teacher, supervisor, principal, neighbour, parent, or older friend.

✓ Do set a good example for others. Be community-minded.

✓ Do treat everyone with respect.

✗ Don't stand by and say nothing.

✗ Don't follow bad examples.

✗ Don't encourage smart-mouths with your admiration.

✗ Don't be intimidated. Change happens one person at a time.

QUIZ

Do you really get it?

So you think you know how to handle just about anything that could come up when dealing with authority. But do you really get it? What would you do in these situations? This quiz has no right or wrong answers, because each situation is unique. Your answers may be different from the ones given below, but they could be right under the circumstances.

1 RUDE DUDE

Your friend Haille got kicked off the school bus for being rude to the driver too many times. He asks you not to tell anyone, and wants you to walk to school with him everyday instead of taking the bus. But if you do that, you can't be completely honest with your parents. What should you do?

- Agree to walk with Haille, but tell him you must be honest with your parents. Lying to your parents is risky and disrespectful.
- Encourage Haille to speak with his parents.
- Encourage Haille to speak with someone about whatever is making him upset.
- Offer to help Haille get back on the bus if he can act respectfully.

2 PAY DAY

You see a teenager bugging a younger kid at school for his lunch money. The little kid is obviously intimidated. You're tempted to do nothing — it's none of your business, right?

Wrong. Your silence will tell the little boy that you don't care.

- If you feel safe, tell the teenager that his behaviour isn't appropriate.
- Tell a teacher what you saw.
- Speak with the younger boy. Ask him if you can help. Encourage him to speak with his teacher or his parents.

3 No Parking Allowed

You're hanging out at the park and a police officer starts hassling two of your friends. They didn't do anything wrong this time, but the last time they were at the park they were being smart-mouths. One of your friends is getting really scared, and the other looks like he's going to makes things worse by talking back again. What should you do?

- Try to calm everyone down. Ask the officer if you can help in some way.
- Suggest the group go somewhere else. Call your parents for help.
- Encourage your friends to be respectful. Apologize for any bad behaviour.

4 Camp Creeps

At camp, your best friend Tanya keeps giving the senior camper a hard time. Tanya says she doesn't have to listen to her because they're almost the same age. The constant bickering is making your vacation miserable. Is there anything you can do?

- Talk to your friend about the senior camper's authority and how difficult it must be for her to lead a bunch of girls so close to her own age.
- Explore Tanya's reasons for rejecting the senior camper's authority. Maybe there is an unresolved conflict you can help her work through.
- Speak to the camp leaders if necessary.

5 Gender Bender

You have noticed that your buddy Paul has trouble with women in authority. He's always talking back to his mom, but not his dad. And though he listens to his male coach, he never listens to his teacher, who's a woman. Is there anything you can do?

- Understand that Paul may believe that men are superior to women — this attitude is sexism and it's wrong.
- Talk to Paul. Tell him what you have noticed about his behaviour. Ask him how he feels about women in authority.
- Suggest Paul speak with a counsellor about his feelings toward women.
- Tell him you won't tolerate his behaviour.

Continues . . .

6 CHRONIC CARE

Your uncle is disabled and uses a wheelchair to get around. He pays a caregiver to help him with his daily chores. You've noticed that the caregiver seems to boss your uncle around. You're wondering: who's the person with the authority?

- Understand that your uncle has hired the caregiver to do a job and should have the authority in this situation.
- Talk to your uncle about what you've observed. He may be feeling powerless because of his physical limitations.
- Offer to help your uncle with his daily chores. That way you can keep an eye on things.
- Respectfully approach the caregiver. Ask if there's anything you can do to help ensure your uncle's needs are met.
- If you are worried that the caregiver might be neglecting or abusing your uncle, get help from a parent or another adult.

7 Boyfriend Bully

One of your friends is treated disrespectfully by her boyfriend. He tells her what to wear, who to hang out with, and even what to say. You suspect he may be physically hurting her as well. Your friend asks you not to tell anyone. What should you do?

- Your friend is being abused and needs your support. Talk to her about how she is feeling. Encourage her to talk about her fears.
- Offer to go with her to get help.
- Give your friend some pamphlets about dating abuse.
- Get help from your parents or a teacher if she doesn't seek assistance.

8 Taunting Teacher

Your teacher picks on one particular student. She yells at him and pokes fun at him for being overweight. The boy never says a word and always looks so sad. Is there anything you can do?

- Speak with the student and ask him about his feelings. Offer to go with him to speak with the teacher.
- If he's too intimidated to speak with the teacher, suggest he see the guidance counsellor or principal for assistance.
- Be his friend — be supportive.

DID YOU KNOW?

- Respecting authority earns trust and confidence.
- Using authority respectfully sets a good example.

9 Bothered Babysitter

Your best friend has a regular Friday-night babysitting job. The child's father often drives her home late at night, and she feels really uncomfortable about the way he looks at her, but she needs to keep the job because her family can't afford to give her pocket money. She asks you what she should do.

- Tell your friend she is smart to try to head off trouble. Suggest that, if she feels safe doing it, she should tell the man he is making her feel uncomfortable.
- Find out if she can ask her parents to pick her up after she finishes babysitting.
- Suggest she quit and find another job — it may be the only way to keep the situation from getting worse.

10 BACKTALK BLUES

Your friend is getting into lots of trouble for his backtalk. He seems to have a lot of anger in him, and mouthing off to anyone in authority seems to be his way of getting it out. What can you do to keep your friend out of trouble?

- Talk to your friend about why he's so angry. Give him an opportunity to talk about any problems he may be experiencing.
- Tell him about your concerns and the problems he's creating for himself with his backtalk.
- Identify and discuss the positive results of respecting authority.
- Encourage him to speak with a counsellor. There are lots of things he can do to deal with his anger — things that won't get him into trouble.

- Studies have shown that kids who respect their parents and teachers are less likely to take risks.
- In 1921, Agnes Macphail was elected the first female member of parliament – one example of a rebel with a cause!

More **Help**

It takes time and practice to learn the skills in this book. There are many ways to deal with authority but only you can know which feels right in each situation. In the end, the best response is the one that keeps you safe.

If you need more information, or someone to talk to, the following resources may be of help.

Helplines

Kids Help Phone (Canada) 1-800-668-6868
Youth Crisis Hotline (USA) 1-800-448-4663

Web sites

KidsHealth: Kidshealth.org/kid/feeling
Kids Help Phone: http://kidshelp.sympatico.ca
Schoolnet.ca
Youthpath.ca

Books

Boy O'Boy by Brian Doyle. Groundwood Books, 2003.
Canadian Leaders by Maxine Trottier. Scholastic, 2004.
Evil Masters: The Frightening World of Tyrants by Laura Scandiffio. Annick Press, 2005.
Famous Dead Canadians by Joanne Standbridge. Scholastic, 2003.
Goon Squad by Michele Martin Bossley. James Lorimer & Co., 2003.
Red-line Blues by Camilla Reghelini Rivers. James Lorimer & Co., 2002.
Red Land, Yellow River: A Story From the Cultural Revolution by Ange Zhang. Groundwood Books, 2004.
Suspended by Robert Rayner. James Lorimer & Co., 2004.
This Can't Be Happening! by Gordon Korman. Scholastic, 2003.
Unusual Heroes by Shane Peacock. Penguin Books, 2002.
The Wizzle War by Gordon Korman. Scholastic, 2003.

Other titles in the Deal With It series:

Arguing: Deal with it word by word by Elaine Slavens, illustrated by Steven Murray.
Authority: Deal with it before it deals with you by Anne Marie Aikins, illustrated by Steven Murray.
Bullying: Deal with it before push comes to shove by Elaine Slavens, illustrated by Brooke Kerrigan.
Competition: Deal with it from start to finish by Mireille Messier, illustrated by Steven Murray.
Fighting: Deal with it without coming to blows by Elaine Slavens, illustrated by Steven Murray
Girlness: Deal with it body and soul by Diane Peters, illustrated by Steven Murray.
Gossip: Deal with it before word gets around by Catherine Rondina, illustrated by Dan Workman.
Guyness: Deal with it body and soul by Steve Pitt, illustrated by Steven Murray.
Misconduct: Deal with it without bending the rules by Anne Marie Aikins, illustrated by Steven Murray.
Peer Pressure: Deal with it without losing your cool by Elaine Slavens, illustrated by Ben Shannon.
Racism: Deal with it before it gets under your skin by Anne Marie Aikins, illustrated by Steven Murray.
Rudeness: Deal with it if you please by Catherine Rondina, illustrated by Dan Workman.

James Lorimer & Company Ltd. acknowledges the support of the Ontario Arts Council. We acknowledge the support of the Government of Canada through the Book Publishing Industry Development Program (BPIDP) for our publishing activities. We acknowledge the support of the Canada Council for the Arts for our publishing program. We acknowledge the support of the Government of Ontario through the Ontario Media Development Corporation's Ontario Book Initiative.

The Canada Council for the Arts | Le Conseil des Arts du Canada
ONTARIO ARTS COUNCIL
CONSEIL DES ARTS DE L'ONTARIO

Design: Blair Kerrigan/Glyphics

Library and Archives Canada Cataloguing in Publication

Aikins, Anne Marie
Authority : deal with it before it deals with you / Anne Marie Aikins; illustrated by Steven Murray.

(Deal with it)
ISBN 1-55028-869-5

1. Authority—Juvenile literature. 2. Conflict management—Juvenile literature. I. Murray, Steven II. Title. III. Series: Deal with it
(Toronto, Ont.)

BF723.A78A34 2005 j303.6'9 C2005-900960-8

James Lorimer & Company Ltd., Publishers
35 Britain Street
Toronto, Ontario
M5A 1R7
www. lorimer.ca

Distributed in the United States by:
Orca Book Publishers
P.O. Box 468 Custer, WA
USA 98240-0468

Printed and bound in China